A GOLDEN BOOK • NEW YORK

T#: 608244

rhcbooks.com

ISBN 978-0-525-64796-6

MANUFACTURED IN CHINA

10 9 8 7 6 5 4 3 2

a Little Golden Book® Collection

CONTENTS

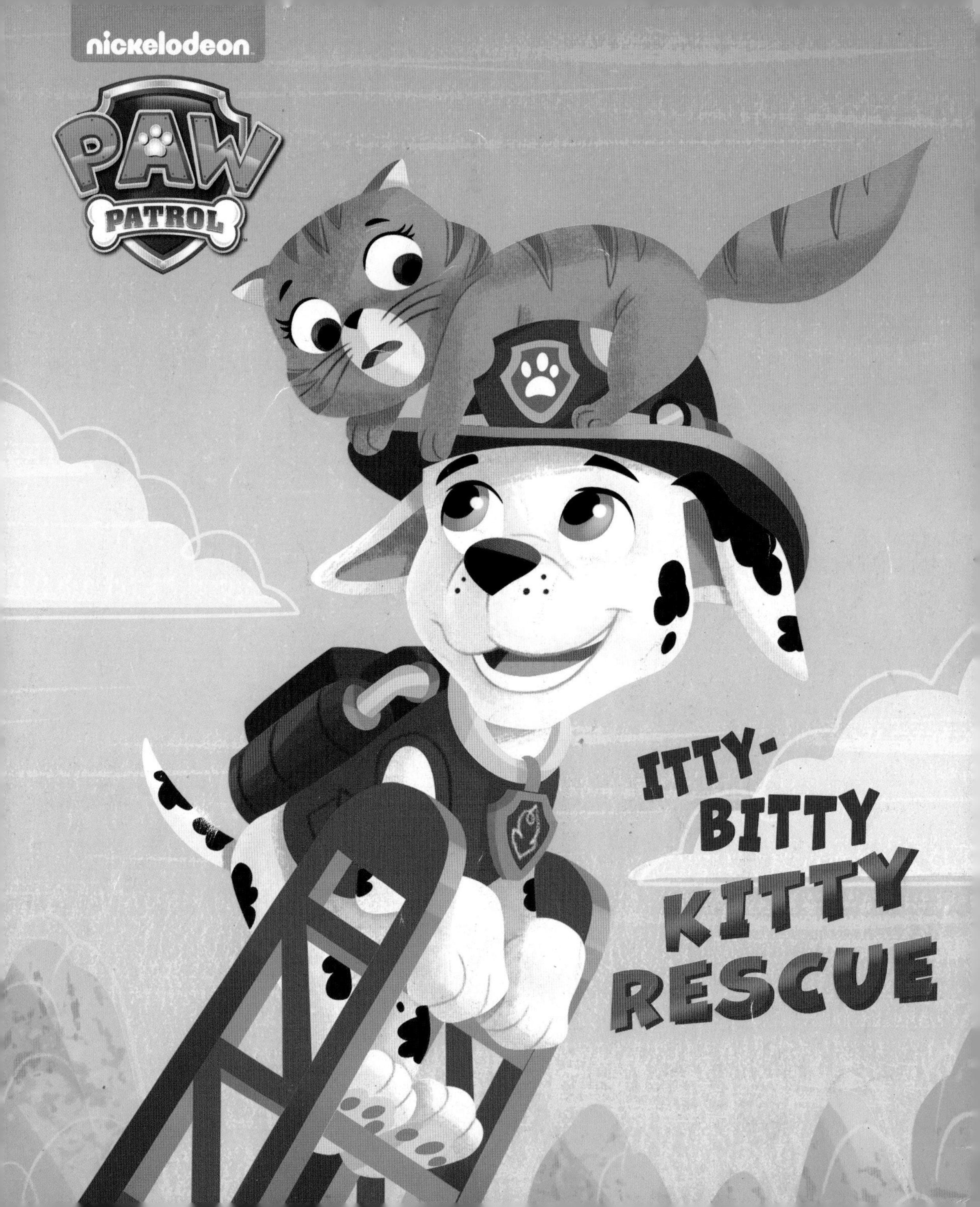
nickelodeon
PAW PATROL
ITTY-BITTY KITTY RESCUE

It was a warm, sunny day. Chase and Rubble were having a great time playing catch at the beach. Then they heard a far-off cry.

"Meow! Meow!"

A kitten was clinging to a toy boat out in the water!

"Uh-oh!" Rubble exclaimed. "That little kitty is in trouble."

"We need to tell Ryder," Chase said.

Chase and Rubble raced to the Lookout to tell Ryder about the kitty.

"No job is too big, no pup is too small!" declared Ryder. He pushed a button on his PupPad and sounded the PAW Patrol Alarm.

Minutes later, Marshall, Skye, Rocky, and Zuma
joined their puppy pals at the Lookout.
    "PAW Patrol is ready for action," reported
Chase, sitting at attention.

"A kitten is floating out to sea," Ryder announced, pointing to the viewing screen behind him.

"We have to save the itty-bitty kitty!" exclaimed Rubble. Then he straightened up and added, "I mean, ahem, we have to save the kitten."

"Zuma, your hovercraft is perfect for a water rescue," Ryder said.

"Ready, set, get wet!" Zuma barked.

"And, Skye," Ryder continued, "I'll need you and your helicopter to help find the kitten quickly."

"This pup's got to fly!" Skye exclaimed.

Zuma's hovercraft splashed across Adventure Bay. Ryder turned his ATV into a Jet Ski and followed. Up above, Sky zoomed through the air. She quickly spotted the kitten.

"We're here to help you," Ryder said, easing his Jet Ski to a stop.

The little kitten jumped from her boat and landed on Zuma's head. The startled pup fell into the water.

Zuma yelled, "Don't touch the—"

The kitten accidentally hit the throttle and raced off on the hovercraft.

The hovercraft zoomed around the bay. Overhead, Skye turned this way and that, trying to follow the hovercraft's twisting course.

"This kitty is making me dizzy," she groaned.

Ryder pulled up next to the hovercraft and jumped on board. He stopped the engine and gently picked up the shivering kitten.

"Everything's all right," he said, pulling a slimy piece of seaweed off the kitten. "Let's take you back to dry land and get you cleaned up."

Later that day, Rubble skateboarded
into Katie's Pet Parlor with his new BFF.
"Aww, whose cute kitty is that?" Katie asked.
"We don't know," Rubble explained. "We
found her on the bay with no collar or tags,
just this purple ribbon."

"Does the kitty-widdy
want a nice warm bath?"
Rubble asked.

"*Meow,*" the kitten replied.

"Do you want me to do it?" Katie asked.
"Cats can be a little tricky to bathe."

"Tricky?" Rubble said. "Not this little sweetie."

But the kitten had other ideas. The moment she touched the water, she jumped away with a screech.

She scurried along shelves, knocking over bottles of shampoo.

Rubble slipped on a spinning bottle.

The kitten fell onto Rubble's skateboard
and rolled out the door!

Down the street from Katie's Pet Parlor, Ryder got a message from Rocky: *"A little girl is looking for her lost kitty named Precious."*

Ryder recognized the kitten in the picture the girl was holding. Before he could say a word, Precious rolled past on Rubble's skateboard. She skated down a hill and disappeared into town.

"Chase, it's time to use your Super Sniffer!"
Ryder said.

Chase needed something with the kitty's scent
on it. Luckily, they had her purple ribbon.

Chase took a deep sniff. "She went that way—
ACHOO! Sorry. Cat hair makes me sneeze."

Sniff, sniff, sniff.

Chase followed the scent until he found Rubble's skateboard at the bottom of the town hall steps.

"Good sniffing," Ryder said.

Ryder and the pups looked around and saw
a shocking sight.
The kitty was inside the town hall bell tower!
Ryder pulled out his PupPad and called for
Marshall and his fire truck.

"I'm all fired up!" Marshall said as his fire truck screeched to a halt in front of the town hall. He arrived at the same time as the kitty's owner.

Ryder told Marshall to put up his ladder. "We need to get the kitten down from that tower."

"I'm on it," Marshall declared. He extended the truck's ladder and carefully started to climb.

Marshall reached the top of the ladder. The scared little kitten was clinging desperately to a rope in the tower.

"I'll get you down safely," Marshall said. "Come here."

"*Meow,*" Precious whimpered.

The kitten jumped from the rope. She tried to grab Marshall's helmet but missed—and clutched his face instead.

"Whoa!" Marshall yelped. He couldn't see!

The ladder shook. Marshall lost his grip. He and the kitten fell off the ladder!

Ryder caught Marshall, and the little kitty tumbled into her owner's arms.

"Precious!" the girl exclaimed. "You're okay! You owe these brave pups a thank-you for all their help."

"Whenever you need us," Ryder said, "just yelp for help!"

PUPPY BIRTHDAY TO YOU!

One windy afternoon in Adventure Bay, a box moved down the street toward Katie's Pet Parlor. But this box wasn't being blown by the wind. *It was creeping down the street on eight paws!*

Suddenly, a big gust blew the box away, revealing Skye and Rubble underneath. They quickly scampered into the shop.

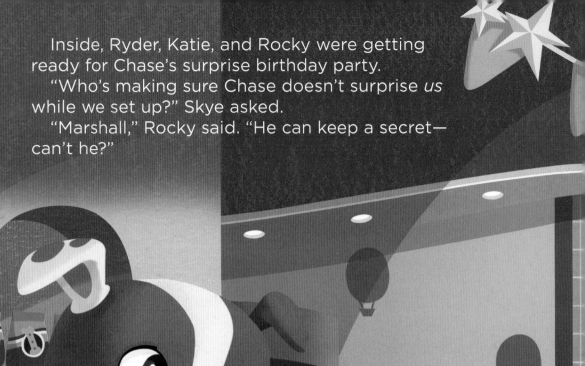

Inside, Ryder, Katie, and Rocky were getting ready for Chase's surprise birthday party.

"Who's making sure Chase doesn't surprise *us* while we set up?" Skye asked.

"Marshall," Rocky said. "He can keep a secret—can't he?"

Across town, Marshall and Chase were playing in Pup Park. They swung on the swings and slid down the slide.

"Maybe we should go find Ryder and the pups," Chase said.

"No!" Marshall protested. "We can't! Because it's, um, so nice out."

Just then, the wind picked up again and blew them right across the park!

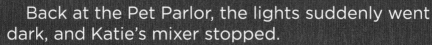

Back at the Pet Parlor, the lights suddenly went dark, and Katie's mixer stopped.

"All the lights on the street are out!" Rocky yelped.

Ryder thought he knew what was wrong. "PAW Patrol, to the Lookout!"

The team raced to the Lookout. But without electricity, the doors wouldn't open. Luckily, Rocky had a screwdriver, which did the trick.

Once they were inside, Ryder used his telescope to check Adventure Bay's windmills. "Just as I thought," he said. "The wind broke a propeller. Since the windmill can't turn, it can't make electricity. We need to fix it!"

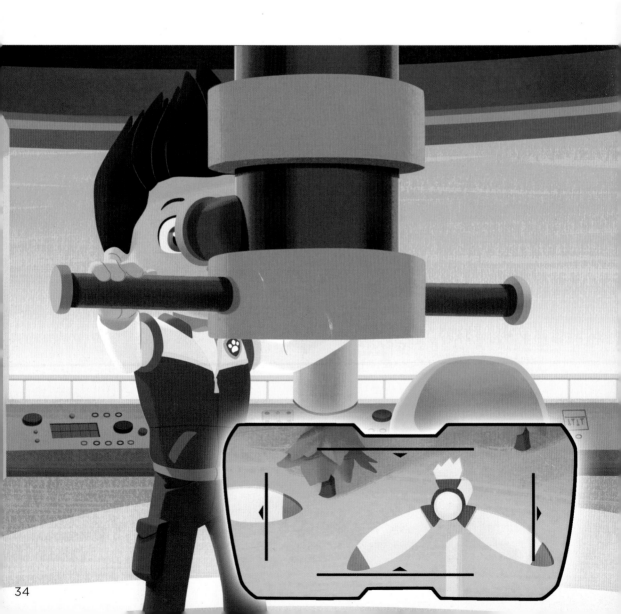

Ryder looked at Rocky. "We'll need something from your truck to fix the broken blade."

"Green means go!" Rocky said, preparing for action.

"We'll need Marshall's ladder to climb up and fix the windmill," said Ryder.

Marshall nodded. "I'm fired up!"

"Chase, the traffic lights won't work without electricity," Ryder continued. "I need you to use your siren and megaphone to direct traffic."

"These paws uphold the laws," Chase declared.

Meanwhile, Skye, Zuma, and Rubble raced back to the Pet Parlor to continue setting up for Chase's surprise party. It was very dark, but Katie had a flashlight.

At the center of town, Chase busily directed traffic.
"You're our hero," Mayor Goodway said as she
crossed the street safely.
"I'm just doing my PAW Patrol duty," Chase said.

Up in the hills, Ryder, Marshall, and Rocky went to work on the broken windmill. Ryder climbed Marshall's ladder and removed the old blade while Rocky looked for a replacement piece.

"No, not a tire . . . not a lawn chair," Rocky said, pulling stuff out of his truck. At last he found what he wanted. "Here it is—my old surfboard!

"This surfboard will catch a breeze and help turn it into electricity," Rocky said as he bolted the board into place. The wind picked up and the windmill started to turn. Lights came on all over Adventure Bay!

The traffic lights started working again.
"Ryder and the PAW Patrol did it!" Chase
announced through his megaphone. "My work
here is done!"

The lights in the Pet Parlor glowed brightly. "Hooray!" cheered Skye, but then she frowned. "Aw! There's no time to make a cake." Katie thought for a moment. "I have an idea!"

As Chase drove back to the Lookout, he got a call from Ryder. "We need you at Katie's— in a hurry!"

When Chase got there, everything was dark and quiet.

Chase stepped inside. The lights went on.
"SURPRISE!" everyone yelled.

Chase was amazed. "Wow! You guys turned the lights back on AND made a party for me?"

"We didn't have time to bake you a real cake," Katie said, "so we hope you like your pup-treat cookie cake."

"Whenever it's your birthday, just yelp for help!" Ryder said with a laugh.
All the puppies cheered and enjoyed a taste of Chase's special cake.

PIRATE PUPS!

One day, while exploring the cliffs above
Adventure Bay, Cap'n Turbot slipped and fell down
a dark hole. At the bottom, he discovered an old
pirate hideout.

   He was stuck in the creepy cavern, but he knew
who could help him: the PAW Patrol!

Ryder called the PAW Patrol to the Lookout and told them about Cap'n Turbot.

"He's stuck in a cavern filled with pirate stuff, and he thinks it might be the hideout of the legendary Captain Blackfur!" Ryder said. "No one knows what he looked like or what happened to his treasure."

Ryder needed Chase and Rubble for the
rescue, but he told the rest of the pups to
be ready, just in case.
Rubble was excited. He really wanted to
be a pirate!

Ryder, Chase, and Rubble raced to the cliffs and found the hole.

"Chase," Ryder said, "I need your winch hook to lower me into the cave."

"Chase is on the case!" He pulled the hook over, and Ryder locked it onto his safety belt.

Chase carefully lowered Ryder into the dark hole.

The pups joined Ryder and Cap'n Turbot down
below. Using Chase's spotlight, they found cool
pirate stuff—a spyglass, a flag, and a real pirate
hat! Ryder put the hat on Rubble's head.
    "Arr!" said Rubble. "Shiver me timbers!"

Chase sniffed the air. "I smell seawater," he said.
He followed the scent and discovered a secret
passage! But it was blocked by rocks.

"That must be the way to the beach," said Ryder.

"Stand back, landlubbers!" said Rubble as he
cleared the way with his digger.

Ryder and the pups followed the passage to a beach. They found an old bottle with part of a map inside it.

"Is it a pirate treasure map?" Rubble asked.

"Could be," said Ryder. "We need all paws on deck to solve this mystery."

Ryder called the rest of the pups to the beach and told them that the map had been torn into three pieces.

"There's a clue to where we'll find the next piece," he said. *"'The part of the map that you seek hides in the big parrot's beak.'"*

The pups thought about the clue. Suddenly,
Rocky said, "Those boulders at the bottom of
Jake's Mountain kind of look like a parrot!"
"Let's check it out," Chase barked.

The team hurried to the rocks that looked like a giant parrot. Skye flew up and found a bottle in its beak. Another piece of the map was inside!

Rocky taped the pieces together, and Ryder read the next clue: "'From atop Parrot Rock, look toward the sea. A clue hides in the hollow of a very big tree.'"

"If we can solve that clue," Ryder said, "we should find Blackfur's treasure!"

Chase thought for a moment. "The biggest trees around are in Little Hooty's forest."

"Good thinking!" Ryder exclaimed.

The forest was filled with lots of big trees, so
Chase asked Little Hooty if he had seen an old
bottle in any of the branches. He had!
Little Hooty fluttered up to a hole high in a tree.

Marshall drove his fire
truck to the base of the tree,
extended the ladder, and
climbed up.
  "Little Hooty was right!"
he said. He took down a
bottle that contained the
last piece of the map.

Rocky taped the pieces together. They now had the whole map! Ryder read the final clue: *"'Walk twenty paces from the tree toward setting sun and rising sea.'"*

Ryder turned to face the sun and the sea, and he started walking.

From the edge of the cliff, Ryder and the pups saw something amazing through the fog.

It was an old pirate ship next to a deserted island!

"Do you think it's Captain Blackfur's ship?" Rubble asked.

The PAW Patrol worked together to pull the ship onto the beach.

News of the find spread through Adventure Bay. Mayor Goodway and her pet chicken, Chickaletta, came to see the exciting discovery.

On board, Ryder, Cap'n Turbot, and the pups
found an old treasure chest. Inside were coins,
jewels, a gold bone, and even a fancy dog bowl.

"Why would a pirate captain have a dog bowl?" Marshall asked.

Then, digging through the treasure, Ryder found an old picture of Captain Blackfur.

71

Captain Blackfur was a pirate pup!
"He looks just like me, except with a *black fur*
beard!" Rubble exclaimed.
The team let out a mighty *"Arr!"*
Three cheers for the pirate pups of the PAW Patrol!

ALL-STAR PUPS!

One morning, the PAW Patrol pups were playing basketball with Mayor Goodway. Skye made a Super Skye Hook right into the hoop! Rocky did his Rocky Spin and Shoot—*swish!* Then it was Marshall's turn.

"Here comes my famous Dalmatian Dunk!" he said, jumping high in the air. But he missed the hoop and bounced right into Foggy Bottom's Mayor Humdinger.

"If you blundering beagles need lessons," grumbled Mayor Humdinger, "my undefeated Foggy Bottom basketball team would be happy to help."

Mayor Goodway folded her arms. "Bring on your Boomers, Mayor. Tomorrow you'll see that Adventure Bay has the top team!"

But Mayor Goodway had forgotten one thing: Adventure Bay didn't have a basketball team. She immediately called Ryder.

"No job is too big, no pup is too small— for basketball!" Ryder declared. "PAW Patrol to the Lookout!"

"We only have one day to get ready," Ryder told the pups at the Lookout. "Chase, I'll need you to use your whistle, megaphone, and traffic cones to help run the practice. Marshall, I'll need you standing by with water and ice to make sure no one gets overheated. The rest of you pups—I need you to be the team!"

Later, at the basketball court, Chase set up a running-and-bouncing drill.

"Okay, team, let's see some hustle!" he said.

As Marshall dribbled the basketball, it bounced out of control and he tripped over the cones.

79

The pups piled into a pyramid next to the hoop. Marshall tried to pass the ball and took a tumble instead! Luckily, Skye nudged the ball into the hoop at the last second.

On the big day, the mayor gave Ryder and the pups a team name: the Adventure Bay All-Stars! But they didn't feel like all-stars. They felt nervous, especially Marshall. "I don't think I should play in the game," he said to Ryder. "If someone gets hurt, I want to be ready."

"Are you sure that's the reason?" asked Ryder.

Marshall nodded, but he was secretly worried that he wasn't good enough to be on the team.

The Adventure Bay All-Stars lined up against the Foggy Bottom Boomers. Rubble and a Boomer faced off at the center.

Cap'n Turbot was the referee. "Okay, players. Let's see super sportsmanship for this sporting spectacle!" He tossed the basketball into the air, and the game was on!

The Boomer leaped up and
knocked the ball away from Rubble.
Foggy Bottom had the advantage!

The ball bounced to a Boomer, who took
a shot—and scored!

"Just let us know when you've had enough,
Mayor Goodway!" chuckled Mayor Humdinger.

At the end of the court, Ryder passed the ball to Rocky. The pup dribbled down the court, dodging Boomers left and right!

Rocky threw the ball to Skye, who flipped it toward the hoop. The Adventure Bay All-Stars and the Foggy Bottom Boomers were tied, 2–2!

The Boomers headed down
the court, and then suddenly,
Zuma stole the ball and passed it
to Ryder. Ryder dribbled, weaved
past a Boomer, shot—and scored!

Up and down the court the players dribbled, shot, and scored . . . and the Adventure Bay All-Stars were winning!

"I can't believe the pups are ahead. . . . I mean, go, All-Stars!" cheered Mayor Goodway.

Mayor Humdinger twirled his mustache and whispered to a Boomer, "You know what to do."

As Rocky and Zuma headed down the court, the Boomer stuck out his foot—and sent them tumbling!

From the sidelines, Marshall raced to the rescue. He bandaged Rocky's sprained paw and put an ice pack on Zuma's tail to keep the swelling down.

"Do you want to play?" Ryder asked Marshall. "We need you. Otherwise, we don't have enough players."

Marshall hung his head. "I'm kind of clumsy with the ball."

"It doesn't matter how good you are—you're a part of our team!" said Chase. "Come on! No game is too big, no pup is too small!"

With Marshall on the team, the All-Stars
trotted onto the court. When Ryder missed
a foul shot, Marshall dove for the rebound,
but a Boomer beat him to it.

Ryder patted Marshall. "Don't worry.
You'll get it next time."

As the clock ticked down to the final seconds, the All-Stars were losing, 43–42.

"Marshall!" called Ryder as he passed the ball to him.

"Whoaaa!" Marshall landed on top of the ball and rolled right past the Boomer defense.

Marshall was still struggling to control the ball. He dove on top of it, and both the ball and the pup bounced high in the air and right into the hoop!

The final buzzer sounded. On the scoreboard, the All-Stars had 44 points and the Boomers had 43. Marshall had scored the winning basket for the Adventure Bay All-Stars!

Ryder reached up to help Marshall down. "Great move, Marshall!"

"You won the game!" cheered Skye.

Ryder smiled. "If you ever need some all-star players, just yelp for help!"

Jurassic Bark!

It was an
exciting day for the
PAW Patrol. They were going on a hunt for
dinosaur bones!
"Are you pup paleontologists primed
for a big dino dig?" asked Cap'n Turbot.

"I'm ready to shovel!" said Rubble.
"We want to find fossils—bones
that are so old, they're hard as rocks,"
Ryder said.

The PAW Patroller rolled up to the dig
site, and the pups went to work.
    While Chase placed traffic cones to
keep the work area safe, Rubble used his
shovel to dig.

"Whoa! My shovel hit something!" exclaimed Rubble.

Cap'n Turbot was amazed at what Rubble had found. "These are a billion times better than dino bones—they're dino *eggs*!"

"Way to dig, Rubble!" said Ryder.

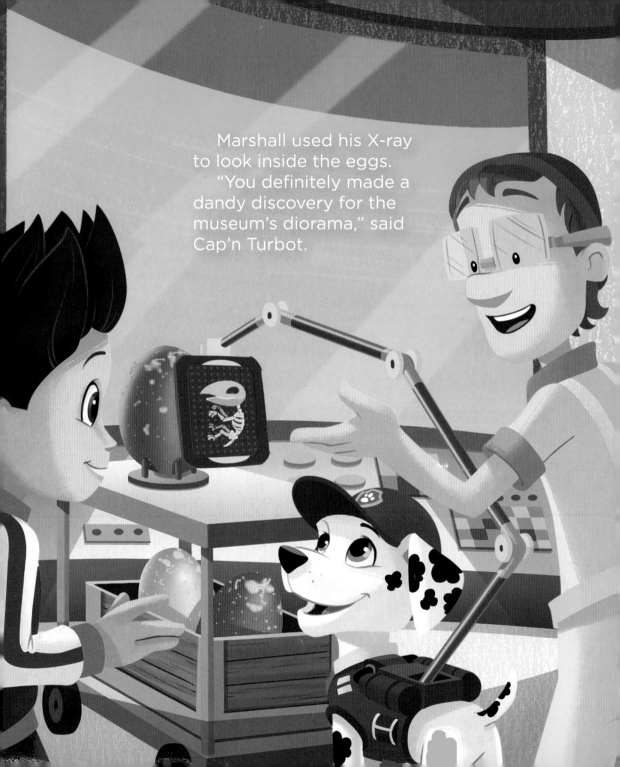

Marshall used his X-ray to look inside the eggs. "You definitely made a dandy discovery for the museum's diorama," said Cap'n Turbot.

Later, the pups tried to guess what was inside the eggs.
"I bet they're pterodactyls," said Marshall.
"Or *pup*-odactyls!" added Skye.

But Rubble was tired from his big day
of digging. "Time for a prehistoric nap,"
he said, and his head filled with dinosaurs
as he began to dream. . . .

Dinosaurs were everywhere in Adventure Bay! A mother pterodactyl built a nest for her three eggs, but one rolled out and landed in a tree.

A triceratops and her child wandered the hills.

And a giant Utahraptor ate Mayor Goodway's lunch!

Rubble was about to rescue the pterodactyl egg in the tree when suddenly, it hatched! The other eggs in the nest hatched, too! Three small flying dinos zoomed into the air.

Rubble had no time to save the pterodactyls because a train was having trouble with a triceratops!

Rubble sped to the stopped
train and found a baby triceratops
resting on the tracks in front of it.
    "Triceratops are my favorite
dinos!" said Rubble. "Let's get you
off the tracks!"

Rubble climbed onto the triceratops's back, and the dinosaur gave him a ride away from the tracks. Then they played with the mother triceratops.

"You did it, Rubble!" exclaimed the engineer. "You saved the day!"

Meanwhile, Marshall found one of the baby
pterodactyls in a tree. He wanted to return it to
its mother. Marshall climbed up his fire ladder—
and the dino bonked him with its beak!
Marshall fell to the ground.

"I'm good!" Marshall
said as the baby flapped
down and landed gently
on his tummy.

Skye arrived in her helicopter and lowered a harness to Marshall. He slipped into it, and as he was carried into the air, he called to the baby pterodactyl, "Follow me!"

The baby dinosaur flew all the way back to its nest with Marshall.

Over at the playground, Chase found another baby pterodactyl. He launched a net from his pack and snagged it.

Just then, the relieved mother pterodactyl flew down. She removed the net and happily took off with her baby.

Not far away, Skye zoomed over Adventure Bay and spotted the last baby pterodactyl. She swooped down to rescue it—and the giant Utahraptor jumped in her way!

"Keep your claws off that baby, you big bully!" Skye barked.

The giant raptor roared through Adventure Bay. It ate all the hamburgers, then swallowed all Mr. Porter's vegetables. It even gobbled up the PAW Patrol's favorite treats, liver links!

Watching this gave Rocky an idea.

A sausage link hit the raptor on the snout.
Then another. And another!
Rocky had turned his truck into a sausage
slinger. As it drove away from Adventure Bay,
it flung links into the air. The Utahraptor followed,
hungrily gulping down the treats.
"It's time to lead this parade out of town
and into the jungle!" said Rocky.

The mother pterodactyl was glad to have her babies back.

"We were happy to help," says Ryder. "Whenever you're in trouble, just squawk for help."

Skye and Marshall took to the air, ready to lead the family to the jungle.

"*Aww*, you guys are going, too?" asked Rubble. The mother and baby triceratops roared goodbye as they lumbered away.

"They'll all be much happier in the jungle," said Ryder.

"Saving dinosaurs sure makes me tired," Rubble said with a yawn, and he stretched out on the grass. . . .

"Wake up, Rubble!" said Cap'n Turbot.
"Nifty news! Those eggs you found are
from a new species no one's ever seen!
I named it Rubble-o-saurus!"

"Wow! Thanks!" said Rubble. He couldn't
believe a dinosaur was now named after
him. It was a dream come true!

SAVE THE
SCHOOL BUS!

One sunny morning, Mr. Hudson,
the school bus driver, was starting his
route through Adventure Bay. Suddenly,
Mr. Porter's delivery truck spilled a big
bunch of bananas! The bananas landed
in front of the school bus, sending
it sliding and skidding off the road.
    There were loud popping sounds as
the bus rolled over some pointy spikes!

All four tires on the bus were flat!
How could Mr. Hudson pick up the
kids and take them to school? He
knew he had to alert the PAW Patrol!

"Don't worry," Ryder said. "No job is too big, no pup is too small!"

Ryder called the pups to the PAW Patroller.

Inside the PAW Patroller, Ryder told the team about the flat tires.

"Rocky, your ratchet and tire-patching gear will get that bus rolling again. Marshall, use your water cannons to spray the squished fruit off the street so no one else skids out."

"But how will the kids get to school on time?" Chase asked. The bell was going to ring in ten minutes!

Ryder thought for a moment.
"We'll just have to use a substitute
school bus—the PAW Patroller!"
    The pups cheered as they
raced to the scene.

Rocky used his forklift to prop up the bus. Then he got to work removing the tires with his ratchet.

At the same time, Marshall hosed down the mush on the road with his water cannons. "Wow!" exclaimed Mr. Hudson. "That's one power-washing pup!"

Meanwhile, Ryder, Chase, and Robo
Dog used the PAW Patroller to pick up
the kids and take them to school. At the
first stop was a boy named Alex.
    "This isn't a school bus—it's a *cool*
bus!" he exclaimed as he got on.

Next, they picked up Julius and Julia.
"Come aboard the temporary bus!"
Chase announced over his loudspeaker.
The brother and sister hurried inside
and took seats.

Just then, Mayor Goodway and her pet chicken, Chickaletta, walked by. "A new school bus!" the mayor exclaimed.

Chickaletta was so excited that she dropped her ear of corn, and it rolled away. She ran after it. Ryder, Robo Dog, and Chase followed her.

The older kids explored the PAW Patroller. Alex climbed into Chase's police truck, Julius pretended to steer Zuma's hovercraft, and Julia sat in Rubble's rig.

Ryder, Chase, and Robo Dog finally returned with Chickaletta, who had retrieved her ear of corn.

Chickaletta started to peck at
the PAW Patroller's control panel.
Then they heard a rumbling noise.

One by one, the pups' vehicles were rolled out onto the road—with the kids inside! Chickaletta had pressed the launch button with her beak!

"Whoa!" yelled Alex.
"Whee!" screamed Julia.
"Woo-hoo!" whooped Julius.

"No, Chickaletta!" said Ryder. But the
poor chicken was so startled that she flew
straight up, landed in Skye's helicopter,
and pecked the control panel there, too!
   The copter's engine started, and away
the chicken flew!

Ryder quickly called the other pups at the Lookout.

"Team," he said, "our school bus rescue has taken a detour! The kids are out riding in your vehicles! We need to get them back."

Skye popped open the wings on her Pup Pack and zoomed up to the chicken flying in her copter.

"Looks like you need a copilot," she said, slipping into the seat next to Chickaletta. Skye grabbed the controller and safely steered the chopper—and its pecking passenger—toward home.

Back on the ground, Rubble raced toward his rig on his skateboard. With a few fancy moves, he flipped himself inside the Digger next to Julia. He pressed the brake, barely avoiding a crash with Mr. Porter's fruit stand.

Out on the water, Julius was speeding toward Cap'n Turbot's boat. Zuma zoomed up to the hovercraft on a kite-powered surfboard and leaped behind the wheel.

The hovercraft turned, missing the boat at the last second!

Meanwhile, Ryder and Chase caught up to Alex.
"Time to pull over," the pup barked.
But Alex didn't know how!
Ryder instructed Chase to shoot a net from his Pup Pack. The net sailed through the air and stretched between two trees, catching the patrol truck like a soccer ball.
"Goal!" Ryder and Chase shouted, high-fiving each other.

Everyone rushed back to the PAW Patroller. If they hurried, they could still get the kids to school on time!

But then the PAW Patroller's door suddenly opened, and a little girl threw out a bouncy ball. Robo Dog chased it while the girl started up the giant vehicle. The PAW Patroller rolled down the street!

Ryder sprang into action.
"Skye, get your copter back in the air and lower the harness!" he said.
Once Ryder had strapped himself into the harness, Skye flew over the PAW Patroller. Ryder dropped down through the roof and ran to the front. He reached for the controls . . .

. . . and brought the vehicle to a
stop in front of the school—just
as the other pups pulled up.
    The bell rang.

The kids waved goodbye and ran inside
as the school bus rumbled up the street
and screeched to a halt. Rocky had fixed
the tires, and the bus was as good as new!
    "Did you just get here?" he asked his
teammates with a giggle. "What took you
so long?"

Adventures with Grandpa!

One day, Ryder and the PAW Patrol were at Mr. Porter's market and restaurant with their friend Alex. Mr. Porter was Alex's grandpa—or, as Alex liked to call him, "the best grandpa ever!"

"I have a special treat for all of you today!" Mr. Porter announced.

"What is it?" Alex asked, jumping up and down excitedly.

Chase took a deep whiff with his super sniffer. "My nose knows! It's cherry pie!"

"And cherry pup treats for the PAW Patrol!"
said Mr. Porter as he served Alex and the team.
"I could never forget our favorite pups!"
He headed back into his restaurant.
   "This is yummy in my tummy!" said Rubble,
licking his lips. "Mr. Porter is such a great baker."
   "And a great grandpa, too!" Alex added.

"We should do something nice for him," Zuma suggested.

"That's a super idea," said Ryder. "What do you think he'd like?"

Alex and the pups thought for a moment.

"Well, he likes to cook," Alex said.
"Yeah!" said Skye. "Remember the pizza party in the mountains?"

"But we almost didn't get there!" Alex recalled. "We were bringing the pizza dough to the party when our delivery truck hit a patch of ice. We nearly slid off the road!"

"That's when I zoomed to the rescue with my copter!" Skye said, remembering. "I lowered the harness . . ."

". . . and I buckled in and became Super Alex!" Alex cheered.

Then Chase pulled the truck back onto the road with his winch. Mr. Porter was glad the pizza ingredients and the truck were safe, but he was even happier that Alex was safe!

"Mr. Porter loves helping you do new things,
Alex," Rocky said. "Remember the time he helped
you make your Super Trike?"

"You guys built the Super Trike using items from the restaurant," Rocky went on. "There was a vegetable crate for a seat and big trays for wheels. Mr. Porter really knows how to reuse and recycle!"

"He taught me everything I know," Alex said proudly.

"And your grandpa likes to go hiking with you,"
Rubble reminded him.

"That's true," Alex said. "We hike in the woods
all the time!"

Marshall helped Skye make a big banner for the party.

"Water cannons ready!" Marshall announced. He used them to squirt paint onto a long sheet.

When it was dry, Skye took it to her helicopter.

After that, Alex worked with Ryder and the rest of the pups on a very special pizza. "Let's make it *pup*-peroni," said Rubble with a giggle.

While the pups drove the food and decorations to the woods, Alex asked his grandpa to go for a hike.

Mr. Porter thought for a moment. "Well, I was just about to close the market, and—"

Alex grabbed his grandpa's hand. "Great! Let's go!"

After they changed into hiking clothes, Alex and his grandpa headed into the forest.

"It's great being with you, Alex," Mr. Porter said.

"I love all the time we spend together, Grandpa," Alex said. "That's why I have a surprise for you. . . ."

The two rounded a bend and found Ryder and the pups waiting with the party all set up.

"Surprise!" they cried.

Skye zoomed overhead in her helicopter. Trailing behind it was a big banner.

I LOVE YOU, GRANDPA!

Mr. Porter was very surprised. He couldn't believe everyone had done this for him. And he was especially surprised by the pizza—it looked like him!